Samuel French Acting Edition

Off Off Broadway Festival Plays 41st Series

clarity
by Korde Arrington Tuttle

The Cleaners
by Lindsay Joy

Grandpa and the Gay Rabbi
by Jonathan Josephson

Monsoon Season
by Lizzie Vieh

Risen from the Dough
by France-Luce Benson

Wedding Bash
by Andrew Leeds & Lindsey Kraft

SAMUELFRENCH.COM   SAMUELFRENCH.CO.UK

ISBN 978-0-573-70613-4

www.SamuelFrench.com
www.SamuelFrench.co.uk

FOR PRODUCTION ENQUIRIES

UNITED STATES AND CANADA
Info@SamuelFrench.com
1-866-598-8449

UNITED KINGDOM AND EUROPE
Plays@SamuelFrench.co.uk
020-7255-4302

Each title is subject to availability from Samuel French, depending upon country of performance. Please be aware that *OFF OFF BROADWAY FESTIVAL PLAYS, 41ST SERIES* may not be licensed by Samuel French in your territory. Professional and amateur producers should contact the nearest Samuel French office or licensing partner to verify availability.

No one shall make any changes in this title(s) for the purpose of production. No part of this book may be reproduced, stored in a retrieval system, or transmitted in any form, by any means, now known or yet to be invented, including mechanical, electronic, photocopying, recording, videotaping, or otherwise, without the prior written permission of the publisher. No one shall upload this title(s), or part of this title(s), to any social media websites.

For all enquiries regarding motion picture, television, and other media rights, please contact Samuel French.

MUSIC USE NOTE

Licensees are solely responsible for obtaining formal written permission from copyright owners to use copyrighted music in the performance of this play and are strongly cautioned to do so. If no such permission is obtained by the licensee, then the licensee must use only original music that the licensee owns and controls. Licensees are solely responsible and liable for all music clearances and shall indemnify the copyright owners of the play(s) and their licensing agent, Samuel French, against any costs, expenses, losses and liabilities arising from the use of music by licensees. Please contact the appropriate music licensing authority in your territory for the rights to any incidental music.

IMPORTANT BILLING AND CREDIT REQUIREMENTS

If you have obtained performance rights to this title, please refer to your licensing agreement for important billing and credit requirements.

The Samuel French Off Off Broadway Short Play Festival started in 1975 and is one of the nation's most established and highly regarded short play festivals. During the course of the Festival's forty-one years, more than five hundred theatre companies and schools participated in the Festival, including companies from coast to coast as well as abroad from Canada, Singapore, and the United Kingdom. Over the years, more than two hundred submitted plays have been published, with many of the participants becoming established, award-winning playwrights.

For more information on the Samuel French Off Off Broadway Short Play Festival, including history, interviews, and more, please visit www.oobfestival.com.

Festival Co-Artistic Directors: Amy Rose Marsh and Casey McLain
Festival Literary Team: Garrett Anderson and Ben Coleman
Literary Coordinator: Emily Sorensen
Dramaturg/Editorial Coordinator: Sarah Weber
Marketing Team: Coryn Carson, Chris Kam, Courtney Kochuba, Ryan Pointer, Andrew Rincón, and Abbie Van Nostrand
Press: Keith Sherman and Associates
Stage Manager: Laura Manos-Hey
House Manager: Tyler Mullen
Festival Staff: Rosemary Bucher, Charles Graytok, Ryan Hendricks, Ryan McLeod, Elizabeth Minski, Kevin Peterson, Theresa Posorske, Nikki Przasnyski, Becca Schlossberg, and Alejandra Venecio
Festival Interns: Suzanne Bronson, Derick Edgren, Clare Livingston, Elisabeth Siegel, and Hannah Tyler

HONORARY GUEST PLAYWRIGHT
Tina Howe

FESTIVAL JUDGES
George Brant
Evan Cabnet
Gretchen Cryer
Michael Gioia
Jen Grigg
Joshua Harmon
Howard Sherman
Crystal Skillman
Jack Smart
Niegel Smith
Rob Weinert-Kendt
Susan Westfall

TABLE OF CONTENTS

FOREWORD

Samuel French is honored to have the seven daring and inspirational playwrights included in this collection as the winners of our 41st Annual Off Off Broadway Short Play Festival. This year our Festival received over 1,400 submissions from around the world. We thank all of these gifted playwrights for sharing their talent with us and welcome each writer into our elite group of Off Off Broadway Festival winners.

We also wish to thank the producing companies who helped stage these works at our Festival. The vital relationship between playwright and theatre is one that we know well at Samuel French. Whether producing a Tony-winning play or developing a new work, theatre companies play a vital role in cultivating new audiences and communicating a playwright's vision. We commend them for this mission and thank each of the producers involved in the 41st Annual Festival for their tireless contribution and dedication to their playwright.

Perhaps the most challenging part of the OOB Festival is our production week. From our initial pool of Final Forty playwrights, we ultimately select six plays for publication and representation by Samuel French. Of course, we can't make our selection alone, so we enlist some brilliant minds within the theatre industry to help us in this process. Each night of the Festival, we have an esteemed group of three judges consisting of a Samuel French playwright and two other members of the theatre industry. We thank them for their support, insight, and commitment to the art of playwriting.

Samuel French is a 187-year-old company rich in history while at the same time dedicated to the future. We are constantly striving to develop ground-breaking methods which will better connect playwright and producer. With a team committed to continuing our tradition of publishing and licensing the best new theatrical works, we are boldly embracing our role in this industry as bridge between playwright and theatre.

On behalf of our board of directors; the entire Samuel French team in our New York, Los Angeles, and London offices; and the over 10,000 playwrights, composers, and lyricists that we publish and represent, we present you with the six winning plays of the 41st Annual Samuel French Off Off Broadway Short Play Festival.

Get ready to be inspired.

Amy Rose Marsh & Casey McLain
Co-Artistic Directors
The Samuel French Off Off Broadway Short Play Festival

clarity

Korde Arrington Tuttle

clarity was produced as part of the Samuel French Off Off Broadway Short Play Festival at the East 13th Street Theater in New York City on August 9, 2016. The production was directed by Stevie Walker-Webb. The cast was as follows:

CAMERON . . . . Reggie D. White

clarity received development support from The Fire This Time Festival.

CHARACTERS

CAMERON – Late 20s to early 30s

SETTING

Savannah, Georgia
Hotel room in the historic district

TIME

The Present

AUTHOR'S NOTES

To suit the needs of the production, wardrobe choices may vary at the top of the play. Excluding the tie, the pace at which Cameron dresses is also subject to change. A bare stage is encouraged.

(*Lights up on a warm, upscale, historic-feeling hotel room, where we find* **CAMERON**: *tall, lean, toned – wearing a backwards fitted cap, clean-fitting button down shirt [yes, it was expensive], tailored dark-wash jeans, sneakers, and a thin, gold chain. His shirt is slightly unbuttoned, allowing his pecs to peer out with ease.*)

CAMERON. Just so we're clear, it was literally the best sex of my life. And just so we're clear, not only does this nigga know how to slang the d. This nigga slangs it with a *capital d.*

(*Beat.*)

Just so we're clear, when that first bead of sweat turned cartwheels down my spine – when I realized it brought *friends?* Big ol' beads of sweat – mondo beads – dripping somersaults down my forehead, doin' the splits down my chest, backflipping the insides of my thighs into silly putty – when I realized this nigga had turned the small of my back into a sweet, saline serenade? *Gurl.*

(*Beat.*)

And this was day one. This was the *lead-in.*

(*Beat.*)

And just so we're clear, it was consensual – I *asked* him to choke me.

(*Beat.*)

His eight thick fingers and two broad thumbs at war with the muscles in my neck – toeing the line between coquettish and combustion – he asked if he was doing it right, hard enough. Sweat beads still flowing – kamikaze-diving into the deep end of our cotton-thread bayou. I told him, I said, "Nigga, make me sound like Whoopie – no, no – Macy Gray circa '99!" And, ya know, he tightened his grip a little bit. "No, bitch, make me sound like a pug!"

CAMERON. "A pug?"

"Yes, bitch. If I ain't wheezin' like my name is Murphy – like I got four legs and no neck 'n' just took a shit on an Upper West Side sidewalk, you ain't grippin' tight enough!" It's hard to find folks who'll really go there, but you know what? This nigga ain't no actor, but he knows how to take direction.

(Beat.)

And *just* so we're clear, when it was over, this nigga held me more closely than attention at a dignitary's funeral. Like hand blown glass. He leaned-in and asked if I know how to spell "paradise" without using any letters. "Like this," he said, and put my right ear to his chest. I let his heartbeat butterfly its way to the tips of my toe nails. And we just laid there like that for weeks. His chest hairs pawing at my cheekbone. My coconut oil and his Degree Arctic Edge deodorant immortalizing the closeness we shared that night.

(Beat.)

And just so we're clear, *that* was the moment I knew I had to marry this nigga. So, I am. This evening at sunset. Here in Savannah, Georgia – well, actually just outside of Savannah. On the beach, out on Tybee Island. There's no doubt I love this nigga. And any opportunity he gets, he makes sure I – and everyone else – knows that *I* am his *person*. And that feels good. To be someone's *person*. But it's also... I mean, I guess I still have – not doubts – doubts is the wrong...look, my heritage – my blackness is important to me. Not just important – it's *essential*. You're lookin' at a nigga who loves niggas and all things niggerish. The multiplicity of our identity – art and style – the music notes quilt-stitched into our laughs – shared struggle.

(Beat.)

And my family doesn't understand – even a lot of my black 'n' brown friends throw shade for...look, I get why they – I do – but I love this nigga. And I unapologetically love myself.

(Beat.)

Just so we're clear, "this nigga" ain't exactly a nigga. He's white.

*(**CAMERON** turns and moves to the wardrobe, where he pulls out a fancy garment bag. He begins to unzip the garment bag, then stops.)*

I haven't seen my Grandma Lucy in... Well, she wasn't exactly thrilled when... But, hey, what are you gonna do? And even though we haven't...in... I called her – out of respect. If it weren't for her, I wouldn't even...

(Beat.)

"Hey, Grandma. Jonathan and I are getting married." Click.

(Beat.)

And it would mean the moon and all the stars and six-to-eight meteor showers, a supernova, and all the water on mars to me – and to him – if you came. That was almost a year ago. Grandma Lucy called this morning. At first, I thought maybe I shouldn't pick up – not the day-of – not today. But I did.

(Beat.)

"Cameron, you there, bae? I prayed on it...and I think it'd be ugly for me not to come."

(Beat.)

She's *actually* coming! As we speak, she's driving down from Columbia. And when I see her – in her little orthopedic pumps – pristine, peppery wig – I'm gonna scoop her up 'n' plant a harvest of love all across those cheeks.

(**CAMERON** *fully unzips the garment bag, revealing a sharp platinum grey, notch-lapel, two-button tuxedo. He returns to the wardrobe, retrieves a pair shoes.* **CAMERON** *either hangs the suit on the wardrobe doorknob or lays it out on the bed.* **CAMERON** *removes his hat and sneakers.*)

CAMERON. And to think – me and my nigga finna to jump the broom! I tried to work out with the wedding planner a way for me to jump the broom and Jonathan just to maybe, like, walk around it? Yeah, not so much.

(*Beat.*)

Next time.

(**CAMERON** *removes his shirt. Places it on the bed just beneath his hat.*)

When Jonathan smiles, it's one of those – he's got one of those Tetris smiles. Whenever he smiles, the pieces just kinda fall into place. And this set of kinda goofy, too-big ears to match his slightly too-big nose, which wondrously balance out one another, and are perfectly proportioned to the size of his too-big...heart. And, gurl, I know you think I've got body, but this nigga got *bawdy*. And he makes me feel like royalty three hundred sixty-six days a year.

(*Beat.*)

Shoot, there ain't gon' be no "next time." If he dies before I do, you gon' have to kill me.

(**CAMERON** *takes off his jeans and places them just beneath his shirt. He dons his dress socks over the following:*)

A list of things he's never said to me:

"You're cute for a black guy."

A reference to anything big and black – aside from my intellect.

"No, it's okay, I can still like you without liking rap music."

"Ya know, Cameron, I'm a minority, too!"

"How are you so fine *and* articulate?"

"Wait, you really like Sufjan Stevens?"

And one of my all-time favorites:

"But what about black-on-black violence!?"

> *(Beat.)*

I don't mean to go on and on like he's some kind of negro whisperer. Is he God's gift to earth? No, absolutely not. But I like to think he's God's gift to me.

> (**CAMERON** *pulls a t-shirt out of a bag.*
> **CAMERON** *puts on his dress pants.*)

Deep down, I recognize that love is love. Or whatever. That it's supposed to transcend race and class and all that other shit. But deep-deep down – in my heart of hearts, I want...black love. I do. A love attached to a history I don't have to have to explain away or justify. To anyone, including myself. A love that doesn't make my little sister feel ugly or my parents feel like failures. Not having to pick-and-choose my battles when he reminds me that he's one of the ones that "get it." A *soul food* type love. A *take a bite outta your shoulder and fill my mouth with amber honey* type love.

> *(Beat.)*

When he held me that first night, when he holds me most nights – my spine is an altar. My eyelashes, sandalwood. Sometimes, when he kisses me on the forehead in the middle of the night, I stir. And smoke from the incense burning in my lungs, it seeps out and fills our bedroom with an ancient, a regal richness. Or so he says. And, ya know, it isn't lost on me that Savannah – that this – is one of the oldest slave ports in the country. A still-serrated tip of the triangular trade. And out on the beach in a little while, as I listen to waves lap the shore, I'll try not to think about blood. I won't think about fractured teeth and saliva, as sea foam speckles the coastline *en plein air* – like an exquisite, forlorn Impressionist work of art.

(**CAMERON** *puts on his undershirt.*)

CAMERON. I've never felt like three-fifths of a person, I've always felt like five. Truth-be-told, times that by two – a bitch always feels like a *ten*.

(**CAMERON** *dons his dress shirt.*)

But maybe when they finally recognized us as whole – a full five-fifths, the cracks weren't smoothed-over well enough and started chipping away at the fault lines. Without even realizing it, maybe it was me – maybe I decided I couldn't spend the rest of my life with another fractured thing. A broken thing.

(*Beat.*)

And gravitated towards someone who's never been three-fifths of a whole. Because that's how I want to be seen. As whole. As someone who people might give a shit about, if I ever died in police custody.

(*Beat.*)

At sunset, I'll stand before a man with eyes that match the very sky under which our union will be consecrated. God – drenched in jewels and a bone-white kufi – will look-on as Gabriel stands at a distance, splashing orange juice and red Kool-Aid into the horizon.

And when it's time to step forward and kiss my husband, will I even be able to move? I know they'll be there, below me – my family. Wriggling mangled fingers up through the sand – peeling back the soles of my shoes, clawing at my ankles, burying chipped fingernails deep into my achilles tendons.

(**CAMERON** *puts on his belt and takes a moment to smooth-out and adjust his outfit.*)

Ya know, every once-in-awhile, when I let myself really go there, I remember that everything hurts. That

– fractured or not – I am and have always been a dying thing. And I feel blessed to have found someone willing to love me in spite of that.

   (Beat.)

And when I think about Grandma Lucy sitting out there in the crowd, I...

   (Beat.)

A couple nights ago, we wanted to do it one last time – as unmarried, non-legally bound, lovestruck folks. Maybe it was the pressure of the ceremony, maybe it was – I don't know – I still can't put my finger on it. But something was different.

   *(**CAMERON** dons his tie.)*

And just so we're clear, entangled in the blissful chaos of it all – sweat beads on suicide missions, bodies, muscles, tongues, sheets, fingers, thumbs, veins, lips – he took his hands and tried to milk all the music from my throat.

   (Beat.)

"I can't breathe," I tried to tell him. But he didn't let up. "I can't breathe. I can't – baby, I can't breathe! Jonathan, ease up! I can't – nigga, I said I can't breathe!"

   *(Stillness. **CAMERON** puts on his jacket. Blackout. When the lights come back up, **CAMERON** is gone. What remains is the image of his hat, shirt, jeans, and shoes laid out on the bed.)*

End of Play

The Cleaners

Lindsay Joy

The Cleaners was produced as part of the Samuel French Off Off Broadway Short Play Festival at the East 13th Street Theater in New York City on August 9, 2016. The production was directed by Michael Padden and produced by James Fauven. The cast was as follows:

JERRY ....Michael Kingsbaker
RITA..Tricia Alexandro

CHARACTERS

JERRY – 30s, of Italian descent. Sweet, awkward, abrupt. Grew up in the Lower East Side of Manhattan

RITA – 30s, of Puerto Rican descent. Tough, fragile, extremely proud, and in a bad way financially. Also grew up in the Lower East Side

(Lights up on **JERRY** *and* **RITA** *in a Manhattan apartment. There is crime scene tape over the door to the bedroom. The rest of the place is sparsely decorated.* **JERRY** *and* **RITA** *are both dressed in bio-recovery suits.* **JERRY** *is struggling as he carries in cleaning equipment.)*

RITA. Where is it?

JERRY. Where is what?

RITA. The stuff...you know, the stuff we're supposed to clean up?

JERRY. Oh, *that* stuff.

RITA. Yeah. Where is it?

JERRY. We'll get to it. My sister said you'd be fine with this. You goosey now?

RITA. Nah. I'm... I'm fine.

(Pause.)

God, it really smells in here.

JERRY. Yeah. A guy died in here. Death stinks. Go grab that bucket.

RITA. *(Scared.)* What's the bucket for?

JERRY. The fucking mop. Go get it.

*(***RITA*** exits into the hallway and comes back with a bucket.)*

RITA. I'm not sure I can do this.

JERRY. Sure ya can. You got kids, yeah?

RITA. Yeah.

JERRY. You clean up their snot and shit and puke and that, yeah?

RITA. Yeah.

JERRY. Well, this is like that. 'Cept it's brains and blood – but, you know, it's like your kids.

RITA. That don't make sense.

JERRY. Sure it does. What I'm sayin' to you is that you clean up foul shit all the time – you just don't think about it. So, the key here: don't think about it.

RITA. You know what happened?

JERRY. What d'ya mean?

RITA. To *him?*

JERRY. He died.

RITA. I know he died. How did he die?

JERRY. You don't want –

RITA. What? They don't tell you?

JERRY. No. You don't wanna know that stuff.

RITA. But, I kinda do.

JERRY. You gotta...oh, what's the word...like, take all the meanin' behind who they were and how they died and put it somewhere else. Like you place it... You separate it.

RITA. Compartmentalize?

JERRY. Yeah! Look at that. You're pretty smart, huh?

RITA. Me? Nah. I just pick up things.

JERRY. I *do* know how he died. I just think it's better you don't know.

RITA. Is it bad?

JERRY. Gun shot. So, yeah. It's pretty bad.

RITA. Gun shot?

JERRY. Yup. You know, Rita, if you're gonna do this – you see a lot of fucked up shit.

RITA. I know.

JERRY. Angie said you needed a job and I always thought you were a great...if you can't handle this, you can tell me. No hard feelings. I'll even pay you for today.

RITA. I need this job, Jer. You know how hard it is to find something with decent pay right now? I got my boys to think about.

JERRY. Right. Okay. I mean, I usually only hire the guys I used to EMT with. They're used to it.

RITA. Nah. I can do this. I just hafta adjust to it is all. I'm a tough cookie.

JERRY. That's what I hear.

RITA. What's that supposed ta mean?

JERRY. People talk.

RITA. What'd they say?

JERRY. That you can be a real ball buster.

RITA. Oh, yeah?

> (**RITA** *puts her hands on her hips.*)

JERRY. I don't think there's anything wrong with that, by the way.

RITA. Good.

JERRY. *(Indicates the bedroom.)* You wanna see what we're dealing with in there? See what we're up against?

RITA. *(Tough.)* Yeah, let's take a look.

> (**JERRY** *carries the mop, bucket, and some supplies into the bedroom offstage.* **RITA** *follows. They are in there for a few seconds and* **RITA** *rushes out. She is clutching her stomach.*)

Ay dios mio.

JERRY. *(From other room.)* You okay?

RITA. I dunno. I...so much...

JERRY. *(From other room.)* Yeah, it's a lot of blood. All the grey matter is kinda in one place though, so we got that goin' for us.

> (**RITA** *starts pacing and breathing in deeply. She is trying to avoid being sick.*)

If you're gonna puke, do it in the hallway. Okay?

RITA. Okay.

JERRY. *(From other room.)* Don't go in the bathroom.

RITA. Why?

JERRY. *(From other room.)* Just don't.

> *(She paces and breathes. She attempts to gain her center back. JERRY re-enters the kitchen. The front of his suit is smeared with blood. There is a small chunk of something clinging to his suit, as well.)*

You okay?

RITA. Yeah, just need a second. You have...you have...

> *(She points to his suit.)*

JERRY. Oh! Nice! Piece of brain. You know what I kinda like about all this? It's the great equalizer. Don't matter if you're black, white, orange, yuppie, homeless – in the end – everybody's stuff looks the same, smells the same. Blood, guts, insides all look – like this.

> *(He throws the piece of brain into a plastic container labeled hazardous.)*

RITA. How are you so calm?

JERRY. Just a part of the process, right? We all gonna die.

RITA. It's so violent.

JERRY. Not all of the calls are like this. Suicide this violent is only every once in a blue moon.

RITA. This was a suicide?

JERRY. *(Ignoring.)* Most of our calls? Decomp. Neighbor smells something funny. She figures the guy in 2A just isn't taking care of his place too good. Smell don't go away. She thinks that maybe a rat died in the wall. Smell still don't go away. Then she thinks – have I seen that guy from 2A? Why no? I haven't. Cuz' he's been dead on his couch for like five weeks.

After they take the body away – nobody knows what to do. They don't want to clean it.

RITA. I always thought the police did this.

JERRY. The police?! What a fucking bunch of clowns! No, they'd botch this shit up.

RITA. How do they know to call you?

JERRY. I'm in the yellow pages. People dying to hire me. Get it?

RITA. *(Like, duh.)* Yeah.

> *(Pause.)*

How do you know it was a suicide?

JERRY. Guy's mom called me. Bad enough to have to bury your son...shouldn't have to clean up his fucking brains on top of it. You know?

RITA. You really help people.

JERRY. This stuff don't bother me.

RITA. What happened? Why'd he do it?

JERRY. Doesn't matter. We just cleanup the mess, Rita.

RITA. Maybe his heart got broken. Bet that's it.

JERRY. Maybe. Who knows. This guy? He's gone. None of that shit matters anymore.

RITA. I bet he was a nice guy...just like, like how he kept his place. All tidy. Nice comforter. Classy. I can tell these things. I'm like a good judge of character.

JERRY. Uh-huh.

RITA. What's that mean?

JERRY. Based on his comforter?

RITA. Yeah. Based on his...

Why didn't you want me to go into the bathroom? He killed himself in the bedroom, right?

JERRY. That's where he ended up.

RITA. But, it was a gunshot. That's pretty friggin' final.

JERRY. You don't want to...you need to disconnect a little, okay? It makes it harder if you... This is why I didn't wanna tell you about how he died.

RITA. I just... I'm curious. I think if I know what happened, then I'll be able to do it. To clean it. Gives me more of a purpose.

JERRY. Ok, Rita. He tried to cut his wrists first. In the bathroom. People don't realize how long it will take to bleed out. So, he wrapped himself up and went into the bedroom and...boom. Done.

RITA. So sad. Imagine what that must have felt like –

JERRY. – No. I don't imagine it. I clean it.

RITA. Right. I wanna see the bathroom.

JERRY. It's through there. You sure you're ready?

RITA. Yeah. I'm better. I gotta get used to it.

> *(She exits into the bathroom. **JERRY** starts to mix some cleaners together into a bucket.)*

JERRY. So...you still live around here?

RITA. *(From the bathroom.)* Yeah.

JERRY. It's a tile bathroom, right?

RITA. *(From the bathroom.)* Yeah, it's tiled.

JERRY. That's good for us – easier to clean.

> *(Pause.)*

Neighborhood's different now – huh?

> *(**RITA** re-enters. She is no longer queasy. She seems to have a new determination about her.)*

RITA. Used to be you didn't go east of first unless you were a smackhead or from Puerto Rico. It was *my* hood. My whole family lived down here.

JERRY. Can't even recognize it now, right?

RITA. Oh yeah – it's all *different* now. My uncle Omar still lives in a rent control place a couple blocks over, and I live down on D. Last two standing.

JERRY. Omar... Omar – oh, yeah. He used to do those barbecues on the weekends, yeah?

RITA. Every Sunday. You went to those barbecues? Omar's?

JERRY. Yeah.

RITA. I don't remember you there.

JERRY. I was there. Just kinda shy is all.

RITA. *(Amused.)* You? Shy?

JERRY. Yeah.

RITA. *(Pause.)* How do I clean what's in the bathroom?

JERRY. Ready to get back on the horse? I like it. Tile is easy.

RITA. You said that.

JERRY. Take this.

(*He hands her a small spray bottle.*)

RITA. What's in here?

JERRY. My own special brew of different enzymes and cleaners. I should patent that shit.

RITA. Why don't you?

JERRY. Too much work. And – a pretty limited market.

RITA. You could market it to other clean-up crews.

JERRY. Yeah, but I don't want them to be as good as us. That's the thing about being number one – you're always looking behind ya. I'd almost rather be number two – always looking ahead...almost.

RITA. You really number one?

JERRY. Yeah, girlie, you better believe it.

(**RITA** *exits back into the bathroom.* **JERRY** *starts to mix up another batch of his "brew.")*

RITA. *(From bathroom.)* You're right about this stuff. Bloods coming out real easy.

JERRY. Told you so. Tile and blood is the best.

RITA. *(From bathroom.)* I don't know about *the best*.

JERRY. What did you think when Angie asked you to work for me? Didja think this was weird?

RITA. *(From bathroom.)* Nah, I thought it paid more than Merry Maids.

JERRY. Fucking A right it does. Hey. How old are your boys now?

RITA. Marco is turning eight next month and Javi is ten.

JERRY. Jesus. I can remember when they were just little things running around Angie's place.

RITA. They're so big now. You wouldn't believe it. Like little men. Javi is gonna be tall – like his dad.

JERRY. Is Chico tall? Thought he was my height.

RITA. Nah – he's way taller than you. He's like six feet. What are you like five-eight?

JERRY. Nine. Five-nine.

> (**RITA** *re-enters. She's holding a sponge and some rags. They are all soaked with blood.*)

RITA. Where do I put this?

> (**JERRY** *points to the hazardous materials bin.*)

JERRY. How ya doing?

RITA. I'm fine. I think.

JERRY. Good. Glad.

> (**JERRY** *looks as though he wants to say more. The silence is awkward.*)

RITA. I'm gonna get back to it then?

> (*She starts to exit.*)

JERRY. Yeah, sure. Hey.

RITA. There something you wanna say?

JERRY. I heard about what Chico did to you.

RITA. What about it?

JERRY. I just wanted to say I was sorry.

RITA. Why you sorry? You didn't do anything.

JERRY. I'm just sorry *he* did that to you. You deserve –

RITA. Better? Yeah, yeah. Look, Jer, I'm... I ain't easy to get along with. I'm a ball buster, remember? Better ain't happening anytime soon.

JERRY. You don't know –

RITA. – I don't need a fuckin' man right now. I needed a job. So, thanks for that.

JERRY. You're welcome. You – I was happy to give you a job, Rita.

RITA. Thanks, Jer.

>*(She exits to the bathroom. He continues to mix. Pause.)*

JERRY. So, you aren't dating anybody right now?

RITA. *(From bathroom.)* Nope.

JERRY. Oh.

>*(**RITA** flies into the door frame of the bathroom, suspicious.)*

RITA. You trying ta ask me out?

JERRY. No. Course not. You wouldn't want that, right?

RITA. You are!

JERRY. – That ain't why I hired you. I just... I always...

RITA. Motherfucker!

JERRY. No. It ain't –

RITA. – You piece of shit. You hired me cuz you wanted ta –

JERRY. – Take you to a movie is all. Like a date.

RITA. Date?

JERRY. Yeah, like I'd woo you.

RITA. Woo me? Jer, you're my boss now.

JERRY. I could fire you. Then, we could –

>*(**RITA** looks stunned.)*

RITA. – I need this –

JERRY. – Didn't mean that. I'm –

RITA. You'd fire me?

JERRY. No. No. That came out wrong.

RITA. – Don't take this away from me, Jer. Don't do this cuz I can't go to the movies with ya. Woo me and shit? Great. Call me in ten years when the boys are out of the house.

JERRY. I would wait if that's what you want.

RITA. You'd wait ten fucking years to take my ass to the movies? You must be hard up.

JERRY. Just forget it.

RITA. You don't wanna date me. Trust me.

JERRY. I... Rita...

RITA. You're a nice guy, Jer. Trust me. You don't wanna –

JERRY. – But I do.

RITA. You don't even know me anymore. You knew me when we were fucking kids –

JERRY. I wanted to then –

RITA. Yeah, right! Nice boy like you asking out a hood rat?

JERRY. I did want to.

RITA. You never said nothing. Angie never –

JERRY. I was SHY. I figured you'd never want to go out with me and I was right, Rita. So, let's just forget I said anything. Okay?

RITA. Fine.

JERRY. Fine.

>   *(They both storm off.* **RITA** *exits into the bathroom.* **JERRY** *exits into the bedroom.)*

(Sticking his head back in.) I'm sorry it even came up.

>   *(Pause.)*

Unprofessional.

RITA. *(Sticking her head back in.)* I'm sorry I called you a motherfucker.

>   *(Pause.)*

Why didn't you ask me when we were kids?

JERRY. You were popular, you know? Out of my league.

RITA. *(She enters furious.)* So, what? I'm in your league now?

JERRY. *(Enters, defensive.)* I said forget it. Let's forget it, okay?

RITA. Well, now I can't forget it.

JERRY. Try harder.

RITA. My life is a mess.

JERRY. Yeah. I know that.

RITA. You still wanna take me out?

JERRY. Mess don't scare me.

RITA. It should.

JERRY. It don't.

> *(He kisses her firmly. She reciprocates and then, breaks away.)*

RITA. Wow.

JERRY. Yup.

RITA. Jerry. I need this job.

JERRY. We just have to clear it through HR and then we're good.

RITA. Who's HR?

JERRY. Me.

> *(**RITA** laughs and tosses the rags into the bin.)*

RITA. Funny. You're funny.

JERRY. You're...

> *(Blurts.)*

Beautiful.

> *(**RITA** looks down at her bio-hazard suit and bloody gloves.)*

RITA. No, I ain't.

JERRY. To me – you are.

RITA. Stop. Shut up.

> *(Pause.)*

So, where ya gonna bring me on our big date? The morgue? The cemetery out in Brooklyn?

JERRY. Nah. I've got a whole wooing process.

RITA. Well, this is what I want. I do wanna see a movie. I haven't been to see a non-kiddo movie in a long time.

JERRY. What kind you like?

> *(She looks down at her suit.)*

RITA. Nothin' too bloody. I like those dopey romantic ones.

JERRY. Yeah? You seemed like an action chick to me.

RITA. Fuck that. You know the one – with that actress? She's like British or something – like all tall and shit. She's all like –

JERRY. No idea.

RITA. Yes you do. I wanna see that one.

And I want popcorn. And Junior Mints.

JERRY. I'll even get you a soda. How's that sound?

(**RITA** *smiles.*)

Now, get back to work.

(*She starts to exit.*)

Rita?

RITA. Yeah?

JERRY. You got some brain on you.

(*He crosses to her and gently pulls the piece of grey matter off. She exits. He crosses to a bio-hazard bucket and throws the grey matter away.* **JERRY** *takes a moment to celebrate.*)

End of Play

Grandpa and the Gay Rabbi

Jonathan Josephson

Grandpa and the Gay Rabbi was produced as part of the Samuel French Off Off Broadway Short Play Festival at the East 13th Street Theater in New York City on August 12, 2016. The production was directed by Jonathan Harper Schlieman. The cast was as follows:

GRANDPA . . . . .Chaz McCormack
RABBI . . . . Ari Shapiro

CHARACTERS

GRANDPA – 70s
RABBI – 30s

SETTING

2009. Rabbi Stein's office at Temple Shalom.

(**GRANDPA** *sits in* **RABBI**'s *office. His walker sits beside him.*)

(*An awkward silence.*)

GRANDPA. When I was young, we used to beat up the gays and take their money.

(*Another awkward silence.*)

RABBI. You seem – surprised. To hear that I'm gay –

GRANDPA. – Ah, well –

RABBI. This shouldn't change anything. I don't know why anything should change about how you feel about me or talk to me –

GRANDPA. Well –

RABBI. Why is anything different? You've been coming to me for weeks, I've been with Temple Shalom for almost two years – It's 2009, a whole new world –

GRANDPA. – I didn't know, so now I know. And I'm, so – I'm. Coping.

RABBI. Coping.

GRANDPA. Isn't that what you said I need to learn how to do?

RABBI. I said that about the passing of your wife, not this.

GRANDPA. This is – this is...in my day, we used to beat up the gays and take their money.

RABBI. Abe –

GRANDPA. It wasn't even a big deal. The Italians beat up on the Irish. The Irish beat up on the Jews, so we beat up the gays.

RABBI. Thank you for the historical context.

GRANDPA. I'm just saying, in my day. Things was... It was Brooklyn in the '40s, it was different.

RABBI. You're processing a lot right now, it's only been a few weeks –

GRANDPA. Did you know Barry Manilow was a gay?

RABBI. …

GRANDPA. My grandson took me to see Barry Manilow, special concert – one night only. He got wheelchair seats – way in the back. It was great. So – it's a special concert, so Barry Manilow stops from time to time to take questions from the audience – and he tells about all kinds of things, where the songs came from, what are his favorite songs, who are his influences – his cantor, did you know that? Did you know Barry Manilow was Jewish?

RABBI. I don't know a lot about Barry Manilow.

GRANDPA. You don't? That surprises me.

RABBI. Can we –

GRANDPA. So I'm raising my hand, and raising my hand, but other people are standing up, you know, and I'm in the very back wheelchair row, so Barry Manilow doesn't see me, never calls on me. So on the way home, my grandson asks how I liked the concert, and I say fine, and my voice is a little hoarse from all the singing, and we're laughing. And he asks me – what question were you gonna ask. I says, I was gonna ask Barry Manilow if he was married. And my grandson says – "Grandpa, you know he's gay, right?" I say – who? And he tells me that Barry Manilow as been married to the same man for 25 years. Well not married, you know gays can't marry.

RABBI. I am aware.

GRANDPA. So that's what he said. Ruined the whole thing.

(*Silence.*)

RABBI. We only have a few minutes left. Did you want to talk about anything else?

GRANDPA. I'm. Trying. To, how you said – cope. I'm working on it.

RABBI. It's not easy.

GRANDPA. I've been spending a lot of time with family, that helps. I used to love being alone, loved it. My wife was so demanding – so demanding, especially the last few years. She didn't cook, she didn't drive, she couldn't dress herself, clean herself, plan anything for herself – doctors. She couldn't do anything. It was hard. Every once and a while, I would babysit the grandkids – go to a ball game – go to the store, alone. And I loved it. None of my kids, not her – no nothing. I loved it. Even when my wife went to the hospital, I could visit, then I could home – alone. Wonderful! I'd watch my movies. You see that Turner Classic ever?

RABBI. Sure.

GRANDPA. You see HBO? I like Larry David, he's funny. Jewish.

RABBI. He's great.

GRANDPA. I didn't understand the documentary about the woman who gave the blowjobs, did you see that?

RABBI. Ummm – No.

GRANDPA. There was this woman, and she made this movie about blowjobs –

RABBI. Can we – can we get back to, what you were saying before?

(A beat.)

GRANDPA. I'm alone, now, a lot. It's – not like it was before, it's different. But I do what I can, I keep up appearances, I sing, I get to the beach when I can. Watch movies. Watch TV, eat. Go out to eat. But, it's…different.

RABBI. You know you're not alone. Your kids, right? The congregation here.

GRANDPA. I like my singing class.

RABBI. Did you join the choir?

GRANDPA. No, gospel choir. I sing at the Mormon Church in Santa Monica. What? The songs are much better. Joyful.

RABBI. Whatever makes you happy.

GRANDPA. I love Christmas songs. I have since I was a kid.

RABBI. You know –

GRANDPA. My father hated that. He broke every one of my records when I was 10.

RABBI. A friend of mine gave me a great CD pack of Chanukah songs, I'll let you borrow it if you want.

GRANDPA. That would be nice.

　　　(A beat.)

So, were you happy when the Dodgers gave the gays a Gay Day?

RABBI. …

GRANDPA. You remember this? A few years ago? When the women were on the, the… Jumbo-screen and they kissed? Women. Two women, kissed. And the Dodgers kicked them out of the game.

RABBI. I remember.

GRANDPA. They threw them out and then there was a whole stink afterwards. And then the Dodgers gave the gays a Gay Day.

RABBI. They – gave the "gays" a Gay Day?

GRANDPA. They gave the gays a Gay Day.

RABBI. How, exactly, did they do that, in your opinion?

GRANDPA. I heard about it on the radio. They gave free tickets to all kinds of gays, and celebrated all kinds of… gay things that day with the free tickets.

RABBI. It was co-sponsored by the Gay and Lesbian Center of Los Angeles.

GRANDPA. Lesbian, yeah. Is that new? Lesbians?

RABBI. The Gay/Straight Alliance Youth Ministry was a part of that as well, in terms of gathering support.

GRANDPA. For all the gays or just the Gay Day?

RABBI. For the women who were treated like criminals despite the fact that they did absolutely nothing wrong.

GRANDPA. I don't think they were robbed –

RABBI. They were put on the Kiss Cam, and they kissed. And then they were kicked out of the Stadium because the fans sitting around them got unruly.

GRANDPA. You know, when I was a kid, we used to beat up the gays and take their money.

RABBI. I would really appreciate it if you would stop saying that.

GRANDPA. But –

RABBI. I know it's true, and your just a harmless old man, but stop bringing it up!

GRANDPA. Okay.

(A beat.)

I heard about Josh, little Joshy. I saw his parents through the window.

RABBI. They're coming to see me, after you.

GRANDPA. That was a terrible. Terrible thing, no one should have to deal with something like that. That isn't the kind of thing we did, in my day. Twist your arm, mess up your hair and your shoes – that's what we did. What happened to that young man –

RABBI. He's twelve. A Child.

GRANDPA. I heard – he was here. When it happened.

RABBI. His family are new members – they joined because of me, because they thought that we were a forward-thinking community and they knew that their son was –

GRANDPA. That way.

RABBI. That their son was gay and that he might be better served with a strong role model. And then this happened.

GRANDPA. But he'll be okay?

RABBI. He was beat up pretty bad. Fractured jaw, and he'll have a scar on his cheek forever. And he was scared shitless.

GRANDPA. That's not right. That's not the kind of thing that we did.

RABBI. Isn't it? How is it different? How is it the least bit different?

GRANDPA. It's different. This was a hate crime, what we did was – it's just what we did!

RABBI. And look at what happened. A whole generation of people grew up to think that that's what you do. They taught their kids as you probably taught yours –

GRANDPA. No, I never did –

RABBI. And now Joshua needs to cancel his bar-mitzvah. Re-schedule it, for at least a year, because he can't talk. His mouth is wired shut. He can't speak – he can't pray. He can't chant from torah. Because of what some other boys "just did."

(*A beat.*)

GRANDPA. If there's anything I can do – for the parents, for the family. Anything.

RABBI. Thank you, I'll pass that along –

GRANDPA. I can sing! You think he likes Mario Lanza? Mel Torme? Jolson?

RABBI. I will pass along your regards.

(*A beat.*)

GRANDPA. Was your dad – gay?

RABBI. No.

GRANDPA. Because I don't know how that happens to a man.

RABBI. It has nothing to do with that.

GRANDPA. Because if I ever – you know, beat him up and… did that to him. I'm sorry. That wasn't nice –

RABBI. My dad isn't gay, you didn't beat him up. No one ever beat up my dad.

GRANDPA. It wasn't a good thing. It wasn't Jewish. It wasn't godly.

RABBI. It's – you shouldn't worry about it. Just live your life openly, with an open mind. That's all God wants. God wants you to be good to people, good to yourself, and loving and open to people.

GRANDPA. God wants me to – open myself to the gays?

RABBI. I think he does.

GRANDPA. You're a good man, Rabbi.

RABBI. Thank you.

GRANDPA. A little young, but that's okay.

RABBI. I won't be young forever.

GRANDPA. You – you have someone?

RABBI. A partner?

GRANDPA. However you say.

RABBI. Yes.

GRANDPA. He's a good man?

RABBI. He is a very good man.

GRANDPA. Makes a good living?

RABBI. Yes. He's a doctor.

GRANDPA. A doctor! Mazel Tov. And Jewish?

RABBI. Yes.

GRANDPA. Good. That's most important. Hold on to him. Hold on to him tight. If that – if he's what makes you happy, hold on to him tight. I like talking to you.

RABBI. I like talking to you too.

GRANDPA. You're very sensitive. Which makes sense.

RABBI. I have another appointment.

GRANDPA. Thank you. And – I'm sorry...if I ever beat up anyone you knew. Good night.

RABBI. Lila Tov. (*"Good Night" in Hebrew.*)

> (**RABBI** *looks up to the heavens, and shakes his head.*)

End of Play

Monsoon Season

Lizzie Vieh

Monsoon Season was produced as part of the Samuel French Off Off Broadway Short Play Festival at the East 13th Street Theater in New York City on August 11, 2016. The production was directed by Kristin McCarthy Parker. The cast was as follows:

DANNY... Richard Thieriot

CHARACTERS

DANNY – In his 30 to 40s. Recently divorced. Works for a technical support company in Phoenix, Arizona.

SETTING

Various locations in Phoenix, Arizona.

TIME

Late summer. The present.

AUTHOR'S NOTES

The * symbol indicates Danny has entered a "microsleep": a brief, unintended loss of consciousness associated with prolonged sleep deprivation. It lasts for only a few seconds and he is not always aware that it has occurred.

DANNY. Julia got to keep the house.

We didn't want to uproot Samantha, and since Julia got to keep her too – Well, they live there now, and I don't.

I got my own apartment.

It's in a building on the edge of the mountain preserve.

It's a motel-style rectangle centered around a shallow pool.

A strip club just opened next door. It's called Peaches. My bedroom window faces its parking lot.

It has a big neon sign. It's five peaches in an arc, kind of like one peach tossed through space in stop-animation. They light up one at a time. It starts with the one on the left, a sort of soft salmon – then peach – then bright pink – then pinkish-red – then the last one – dark red. The red one holds for a few seconds – then the sequence starts over.

I don't have blinds yet.

So all night there's this wash of pink and red sweeping across my bedroom.

I'm not sleeping well.

  *

Doctor Miller tells me they're called "microsleeps." A result of prolonged sleep deprivation. I don't know when I'm having them, but suddenly I'm veering off the side of the road or I've typed gibberish for half a page. She started to go into more clinical detail, but I zoned out somewhere around "dissociative fugue state."

  *

(**DANNY** *in his cubicle.*)

Hi Jodi, I'm Danny, come on in.

How's your first day going? It gets easier.

We're cubicle buddies, so if you need anything, just pop your head over.

It's pretty simple really.

Memorize your scripts.

I mean, you can go off script if you want. You're a human being. But you probably won't need to.

How about I take a few calls, let you listen, get a feel for what we do. Sound good?

> (**DANNY** *puts on a phone headset and answers a call.*)

DANNY. Good afternoon, Southwest Network Solutions, this is Danny.

May I have your name?

That's Ann – A-N-N – Goodman – G-O-O-D-M-A-N – Oh, Ann with an E – that's interesting.

And what seems to be the problem?

Your agents cannot make or receive any telephone calls. That is a problem, isn't it.

What kind of system do you have?

AmbiTrax500 – uh oh, not the AmbiTrax. If I had a nickel for every – Time *is* money, I've heard that.

Have you tried turning the system off and turning it on again?

I have to ask. It's the Miranda Rights of technical support.

I'm going to have to ask you to do it again.

I'll wait.

> (*Brief pause.*)

It's working...?

Well there we go! Isn't that –

Hello? ...Anne?

(Loud thunk – a bird flies into the window.
DANNY *screams.)*

It's okay. It's just a bird.
It's a glass building – they fly into it all the time.
Especially during monsoon season. Heat lightning, electrical storms – they go berserk.

Oh yeah, we've all been talking about that.
Only two blocks over. Sports Authority parking lot, by the dumpster.
Paper said it's drug-related. Removing the head – that's usually a cartel activity. Makes it harder to identify the body.
Know what I think?
The head'll show up.
This dry climate – it's not gonna decompose.

Phoenix is a lot like Ancient Egypt. The dry air – it's why mummies are so well preserved.
That head'll show up.
You can count on it.

*

*(**DANNY** is on his cell phone in the Peaches parking lot. He is drunk.)*

I was only twenty minutes late, Jules.
I understand that's a long time to a five-year old, but I left with plenty of –
There was an accident on the 101, it was grid-lock –
I haven't seen her in over two weeks –
You know last time I went to hug her she pulled away?
Like she didn't know me?
Do you know what that does to me?
That's a knife in my guts.

Yeah, a little.
I was angry, I was upset, I went to a bar.
I'm in the parking lot.

I'm *not* driving home, it's next door to my apartment.

Did I have dinner...? Why do you *care*?

I don't know... I don't weigh myself. Twenty pounds?
Twenty-five?

DANNY. Why *should* I eat?

Why should I sleep?

Why should I get out of bed?

I love you.

So what. It's true.

I'll do anything.

> (**DANNY** *listens.*)

> (*His face changes.*)

Whoa whoa whoa...

What guy?

Keith? That guy who fixed the screen door?

That's not how you introduced him, you never said...

No.

No.

That is not allowed.

I do not allow that.

I will... I will evict him.

I will come over.

I will remove him.

I will drag him out of my house and pop his skull like a
fucking grape.

He does not get to live in my house.

He does not get to live with my family.

Julia...? Julia?

> (**DANNY**'s *nose starts to bleed. He touches his
> nose.*)

> (*His hand has blood on it.*)

> *

(At Peaches. It's loud.)

Chrissy, that's a pretty name, is that short for Christine? Christina, nice, even better.

You girls worked here long? I said, have you – can you hear anything in here? You're young, how old are you anyway?

Summer I was twenty-two, I worked construction and me and my buddy Mike Lippinlaw went to the gym every night after work. I could bench-press one-sixty back then.

One-sixty.

One. Sixty.

It's pretty good.

It's not bad.

It's okay.

You girls working late tonight? Doing anything after?

I said are you working late, maybe you wanna do anything after?

I said are you –

I said I keep having a nightmare where my wife tosses me a water balloon full of blood.

I haven't had sex in eight months.

What?

*

(**DANNY** *is at the grocery store, staring into the glass door of the freezer section. He holds a basketball. He has a bloody nose.*)

Frozen peaches.

Frozen grapes.

Frozen mixed fruit.

(Sees his reflection, startled.)

God, is that *me?*

Oh sorry, I'm talking out loud.

Ever look through the glass, but then you refocus your eyes and see your reflection in the glass? And you're not prepared for what you see? For your own appearance?

Like, why am I holding a basketball?

How did I get here? Why do I have this?

I'm kidding.

It's for my daughter.

She loves the Suns.

Sure, sorry, I didn't realize I was in your way. Get your frozen fruit.

Careful – I have this fear when I reach my hand into the freezer that a hand will grab mine from the other side and pull me in.

I could pop this basketball like a grape.

    *

(**DANNY** *on the phone at work.*)

DANNY. – The Alt button on the control panel.

It's in the lower left-hand corner.

It's a red rectangular button.

It says Alt.

Red.

Rectangle.

Alt.

When it's on it turns red.

It's red?

Good.

You've got the hanger?

You've untwisted it?

I want you to take the end of the hanger and stick it in the space between the button and the plastic edge.

Push harder.

Now I need you to pour the water bottle over the control panel.

*

(**DANNY** *outside Peaches.*)

I didn't hurt her, I grabbed her arm cause she took twenty bucks out of my pocket – could you – please, just let me back in, it's not a big deal, I'm not gonna – *God...*

You are the biggest fucking man I've ever seen, what do you weigh, 350? 400 pounds?

I bet everyone thinks you're so tough but maybe you're not, maybe you're not tough at all, and you know the only thing that's worse than being a guy who looks like a big tough motherfucker but who's actually weak and vulnerable? It's being a guy who looks weak and vulnerable and is also weak and vulnerable.

And the funny part is, in another world, maybe you and me coulda been friends. Me, you, and your big bald head. But it's too late now. We're too far down this path –

What did you just say to me?

Do not. Tell me. To sleep it off.

It is far, far too late to sleep it off.

If I charged you right now would you have to kill me?

*

(**DANNY** *crouches in the driveway of his old house.*)

That's why Mommy doesn't want you to see me, cause she doesn't want you to be scared. But you're not scared. It's just Dad. Sammy's not scared.

Pink chalk! That's the best chalk! What'd you draw?

I can see from here, I like it here by the garbage can, it's so hot out, I wanna stay in the shade.

It's an arrow, and it points toward – Mommy's car. That's great! And another arrow and it's pointing toward –

Uh huh. That car.

Sammy. Come here. I need you to listen, cause your mom might look outside, and –
Come here.

We used to get ice cream on Sundays but now your mom is...the point is, even if I'm not around, you gotta know that it's not because I – it's not about you, and it's never cause I don't love you as absolutely much as it is possible for a dad to love, cause I do, it's just that – um – your dad's been –

She's looking. Run inside. Go.

     *

    (**DANNY** *in the parking lot at Keith's office.*)

DANNY. Hi Keith.
Working late?
I've been waiting a long time.
I knew it was your car cause I've seen it parked in front of my house.
I can see my daughter's sweatshirt in the back seat.
How's my life? I ask cause you're living my life.
Don't mind that. It bleeds all the time. Ignore it. I do.
Come here.

     *

    (*Pouring rain. Thunder and lightning.* **DANNY** *holds something.*)

Imagine a basketball...not heavy enough...a basketball full of sand. It's wrapped in plastic bags. Monsoon season, it's pouring, there's a flash flood in the ravine behind the strip club. A dry ditch is now a raging river. It's dark, but there's flashes of pink and red from the neon sign. You hold it. You feel its weight. Take it in so you can forget it forever. Then – toss. It arcs in slow motion – stop-animation – like a peach. Like a grape. Pink. Peach. Red. Hold at red. Splash. Gone.

End of Play

Risen from the Dough

France-Luce Benson

Risen from the Dough was produced as part of the Samuel French Off Off Broadway Short Play Festival at the East 13th Street Theater in New York City on August 11, 2016. The production was directed by Pirronne Yousefzadeh. The cast was as follows:

MARYSE . . . . Erin Cherry
LEONIDE . . . . Antu Yacob

CHARACTERS

MARYSE – Late 30s to early 40s; strong willed, Haitian-American woman

LEONIDE – Her sister; a few years younger

SETTING

Miami, Florida
A small bakery on in Little Haiti

TIME

Time is the present.

(At rise: **MARYSE** *violently kneads dough with her bare hands. It is hard to manipulate. She picks it up and slams it down on the table repeatedly.)*

MARYSE. *Fout!*

*(***LEONIDE*** *enters with a rolling pin.* **MARYSE** *does not see or hear her.)*

LEONIDE. May? *(Pronounced MY.)*

MARYSE. Damn. Shit! *(Pronounced shyet.)!*

LEONIDE. May.

MARYSE.	**LEONIDE.**
AY YI YI!	MAY!

MARYSE. What! What is it, Leonide?

LEONIDE. *(Extending the rolling pin sheepishly.)* I find it.

MARYSE. *(Grabbing the pin from her.)* Hm! *Merci.*

*(***MARYSE*** *rolls the dough,* **LEONIDE** *stares at her.)*

For God sake, what are you staring at? En?

LEONIDE. Nothing. It's just... You don't think we should... make sure things are in order?

*(***MARYSE*** *ignores her.)*

May, it has been two weeks. Two weeks! They said they would come for another inspection in two weeks, en. That means any day now –

MARYSE. I know how to count.

LEONIDE. – Any day now someone will be here –

MARYSE. I don't care.

LEONIDE. – If we don't have everything in order they will shut –

MARYSE. They won't! Nobody ever make me to do what I don't want to do.

LEONIDE. Yes, I know.

MARYSE. I run my business the way I want. I cook and clean the way I cook and clean all my life. They way my *mere* –

LEONIDE. *Your* mother?

MARYSE. *Our mere.* I do every thing just the way Mami show us in Haiti, en. Did anyone ever get sick from our hands? We are not dirty people.

LEONIDE. They never say we were dirty, they only ask that we use one sink just for hand washing –

MARYSE. I wash my hands. Ah!

LEONIDE. Yes, I know, May.

> *(Crossing to a sink in upstage corner; cleaning up.)*

But must you also leave your coffee here each morning? And even the shells from the eggs you make for breakfast?

MARYSE. I must finish this order before noon. I will clean later.

LEONIDE. And you still have not bought the soap dispenser?

MARYSE. You don't see how busy I am? I will buy it tomorrow.

LEONIDE. Tomorrow, tomorrow, later, later. And what if they were to come in just now. That is already ten points –

MARYSE. *B'um report, en!* I don't care about any points. We work like *esclave* to finally have a place to claim as our own in this country. Now nobody can say to me, "Go back where you came from." Because I have business here. Me and Fritz, God rest his soul, swear to *Bon Dieu* we would have our own business one day so that we won't have to work for these racist devils who think all Haitian people are too dirty and too lazy to –

LEONIDE. *(Throwing her hands up.) Menzami*. You are impossible.

MARYSE. You don't remember all the years we cook and clean for the those white devils?

LEONIDE. They were not devils.

(**MARYSE** *sucks her teeth.*)

And they were not *all* white.

MARYSE. Hm! Those Cubans, always talking in Spanish when we come in the room. I know what they were saying about me.

LEONIDE. Oh yeah? *Habla español?*

MARYSE. Trust me, I know. And the Jamaican family in Pembroke Pine?

LEONIDE. The Thomas? They were not Jamaican.

MARYSE. She have a great-grandmother who was born in Jamaica. She told me herself.

LEONIDE. So what?

MARYSE. So now because she marry a white man she think she is better than me? Pretending they are so good people. Pretending they would never associate with low-class people, and pretending those wild children of theirs were not smoking marijuana cigarette every day. You can smell it a mile away. And she accuse me of voodoo.

LEONIDE. She never said that.

MARYSE. It was in the way she said it. Asking if *I* light this candle, asking, *"What is the purpose of this candle"?* The purpose of the candle, you damn beetch, is to cover the smell of marijuana cigarette from your *vakabon* chidren!

LEONIDE. Okey, okey, forget I said –

MARYSE. And don't let me start with the Black American.

LEONIDE. *Menzami...*

MARYSE. The Black Americans were the worst! They think because they have a little money they are better then me? If it was not for those Black American men –

LEONIDE. May?

MARYSE. – Those *vakabon*, with their pants down to their feet, crazy for their gold and their sneakers! If it was not for them –

LEONIDE. May, you are shaking.

MARYSE. Fritz would still be alive!

I have held my tongue for seven years, en. Seven years! This place is as much his as it is ours.

LEONIDE. Yes. He would be very proud.

MARYSE. I don't care about any inspection. Not today. I trust in God.

LEONIDE. God does not work for the Miami Dade Department of Health.

MARYSE. But I work for God.

   (Pause.)

How long does it take you to chop *epis?*

   *(**LEONIDE** crosses to chopping board with onions, celery, etc.)*

Beside, they will not come today. Fritz tell me himself.

LEONIDE. So you are speaking to the dead now?

MARYSE. Every year, on the eve of his death, he speak to me in my dream.

LEONIDE. On the eve –? Is today –?

MARYSE. My hands, they will not stop shaking. They will not come today.

   *(**MARYSE** exits. **LEONIDE** nervously tries to work. She picks up the knife, then hesitates. She brings it to her nose, studies it carefully. She looks down at a bucket of water near the table. She smells the water, then takes out a chlorine test strip from her pocket. **MARYSE***

> *enters with a cup of water. Just as* **LEONIDE**
> *dips the strip in the water –.)*

That is not *necessaire*, en.

LEONIDE. *(Hiding the strip.)* Pardon?

MARYSE. The chlorine solution. You think I don't know what you are doing?

LEONIDE. I-I just –

MARYSE. There is no need to test it, I mix it myself. What? You don't trust me?

LEONIDE. You think I do not trust my own blood? If you say it is good, it is good.

MARYSE. Good.

LEONIDE. Good. But if it is good, then you should not care if I test.

MARYSE. I care that my own sister does not trust me.

LEONIDE. *Depi kilé?* Since when I do not trust you?

MARYSE. Since the devil Americans send their spy in here –

LEONIDE. He was from the Health Department. No spy. You crazy?

MARYSE. Hm! And who send him here?

LEONIDE. *K'om fe kone?* He was not *sent* here, they go to everybody.

MARYSE. Non, *monchere*. Not the Deli on 52 Street. You know the one. Just around the corner from –

MARYSE AND LEONIDE. Second Ave –

MARYSE. *Exactement!* They have no air condition, no fan, and you can taste the salty sweat in every thing they cook. Even the cat is sweating. *C'est vrai.* I see the cat lick the sweat from his *pee-jon* on the same table where they make their *Medianoche.* Or what about the place we passed on Biscayne Boulevard. Do you remember?

LEONIDE. *(With disgust.)* Rosa's.

MARYSE. Yes. Rosa's. I watch her, with my own eyes, cook a pumpkin soup in a pot I would not clean my feet in. And I see her fry beans in a pan as dirty as the devil's ears. But do you ever see any Health Department making trouble for them? Do you?

LEONIDE. I think –

MARYSE. *Non!* You have not and you will not. You know why?

(**MARYSE** *points to her skin.*)

LEONIDE. Madame Rosa is darker then you.

MARYSE. But she is Cuban.

LEONIDE. No, no. Madame Rosa is Dominicana.

MARYSE. Oh! Even worse. She is not Haitian. They will always give us Haitians a hard time. They will always try to keep us down –

LEONIDE. So go back to Haiti.

MARYSE. He-heeey?

LEONIDE. If you are so miserable here, go back. Go back to no water, no *kurant*. En? And you can have light and cool air when the government see fit. And you know the government in Haiti would have killed Fritz long before if he did not come here –

MARYSE. How can you say that to me?! Today of all days.

LEONIDE. Because it is the truth.

MARYSE. Well the government is not like that anymore.

LEONIDE. So go back!

MARYSE. I have earned my place here.

LEONIDE. Then be grateful.

MARYSE. For what?

LEONIDE. You have business. Your children go to good school. What more do you want?

MARYSE. MY HUSBAND! Did he ever harm anyone? He work good job in the hotel, and provide good life for me, and Robert, and Magdala. And you. He give you a home with us when you had no place to go, en. He risk his life, come here alone, to prepare a place for us. And this place never welcome him. We were never welcome –

LEONIDE. But you are here.

MARYSE. He never bother a soul. One night, he is leaving hotel in Coconut Grove, away from the nice cars, and the young people looking for good time. He walk to Grand Ave to wait for the bus, en. He wait for the bus because he give the car to me. He did not want me to take the Metro downtown to North Miami, even when I tell him how many people do the same thing. No, he say, "I want you to be safe. The children have only one *mere*." So he leave the car for me and he wait for the bus on Grand Avenue. Grand Avenue. What was he thinking? What was I thinking? How can I let him take a bus on Grand Ave at one in the morning? Of course it is not safe. Of course he see someone in trouble. And Fritz was such a good man, of course, he try to help. He try to find police, but they ignore him. They say, "Speak English! Speak English."

LEONIDE. Please May –

MARYSE. Before Fritz die, he tell me what those men...what they did to him...those men...they follow him and... those...men...

LEONIDE. Enough...

MARYSE. ... *Vakabon* evil men...

LEONIDE. God can hear you, en...

MARYSE. American –

LEONIDE. ENOUGH! God knows how your heart beats today, Maryse. But you and I know the truth about Fritz killers. En? They were not American. They were Haitian. Haitian, just like you, and me, and –

MARYSE. They were not like us! I will never forget where I come from. I will never try so hard to be like the people here, who want nothing more then to send me back, that I betray my own people. Those men, those –

LEONIDE. Boys. They were boys.

MARYSE. I don't care how old they were.

LEONIDE. Children.

MARYSE. Those...*children*...try so hard to erase their culture that they become...zombies. With no soul. No past. No sense of pride. I will not be like them.

LEONIDE. And you think a soap dispenser will erase your culture?

MARYSE. It is not the way we do things. The way that man investigate us –

LEONIDE. He was only doing his job.

MARYSE. Turning his nose up, like to say that we smell. Looking at us like we are not human.

LEONIDE. You imagine too much.

MARYSE. Like we are animals. When he, they were the animals. Those men –

LEONIDE. – Are in prison.

MARYSE. AND WHERE IS FRITZ? WHERE IS HE?

LEONIDE. Oh May –

MARYSE. Everything here is just the way Fritz describe to me when we dream together of this place. I see him everywhere. And I see our home. Our home in Port-au-Prince. It is as if he never left. If I start to change then –

LEONIDE. He will still be here. In the smell of the cod fish. In the sounds of spices frying on the pan. Here, in the dough. Here. *(Resting her hand on* **MARYSE***'s heart.)*

MARYSE. It beats heavy today, en? *Si tu plait*, get my bag from inside.

> *(***LEONIDE*** exits.* **MARYSE** *kneads the dough, gently and lovingly.)*

Is it true, Fritz?

> *(Pause. She reaches down to retrieve a pan of griyo. She peels the back the aluminum foil cover; takes in scent.)*

Your favorite. May I?

> *(She inserts a morsel into her mouth.)*

Mm-mm-MM! Ah, *mon cher,* it *is* true. You *are* here, en. Well then, I will fight to keep you here.

> *(She returns the pan to the oven.* **LEONIDE** *enters with the bag and hands it to* **MARYSE.** **MARYSE** *takes out a soap dispenser and hands it to* **LEONIDE.***)*

LEONIDE. *(Overjoyed.)* Ooooh, Maryse...

MARYSE. Where is the book?

LEONIDE. Over there.

MARYSE. Well give it to me!

> *(***LEONIDE** *does.)*

(Flipping through pages.) Now, let me see.

> *(Reading.)*

"*In accordance with the United States...*"

LEONIDE. Is that *griyo* I smell?

MARYSE. I made it special.

> *(***MARYSE** *inhales, taking in the smell. She looks up and smiles as the lights fade to black.)*

End of Play

Wedding Bash

Andrew Leeds & Lindsey Kraft

Wedding Bash was produced as part of the Samuel French Off Off Broadway Short Play Festival at the East 13th Street Theater in New York City on August 12, 2016. The production was directed by Andrew Leeds and Lindsey Kraft. The cast was as follows:

LONNY	Timm Sharp
DANA	Joanna Leeds
EDI	Gloria Calderon-Kellett
ALAN	Richie Keen

CHARACTERS

LONNY
DANA
EDI
ALAN

SETTING

Sherman Oaks, California

(The lights fade up on the living room / dining room of a cozy, well-decorated home in Sherman Oaks, California. Stage right, there's a dining table and four chairs. Stage left is the living room area with a sofa, two chairs, and a large, beautiful, mid-century, walnut coffee table. Upstage center between the two areas is the front door of the house. Upstage right is an exit to the kitchen.)

*(**DANA** is setting the table. **LONNY** is off stage in the kitchen.)*

LONNY. *(Off stage.)* Babe!

DANA. What?!

LONNY. *(Off stage.)* I'm using the new platter!

DANA. Yeah, you know what? Grab the, uh...grab the silver ladle. Edi got us that.

*(**DANA** brings a stack of coasters over to the coffee table. Lonny pops in with a ladle in his hand.)*

LONNY. This thing? What else did she get us?

DANA. Nothing. That was it.

LONNY. How much?

DANA. Like seventy-nine bucks.

LONNY. I thought she was doing well.

DANA. *(Disappointed, shaking her head.)* I know.

*(As **LONNY** exits, **DANA** notices a small mark on the coffee table, and gently polishes it away.)*

LONNY. *(Off stage.)* What'd Alan get us?

DANA. The Margaritaville blender.

LONNY. *(Popping back in.)* What is that? That wasn't on the registry.

DANA. It's fine. We returned it for the cash.

LONNY. How much?

DANA. Three hundred.

LONNY. That was nice. Alan's a nice guy.

DANA. Alan's the best.

> *(The doorbell rings.* **LONNY** *heads for the front door and opens it, revealing a very enthusiastic and pregnant* **EDI.***)*

EDI. Oh my god! You guys!

DANA. Look at you.

LONNY. *(Hugging* **EDI.***)* You're huge.

DANA. *(Quickly correcting.)* And glowing.

EDI. *(Hugging* **DANA.***)* What a wedding!

LONNY. We nailed it, right?

EDI. You killed it. *(Noticing, moved.)* Oh, is that my ladle?

LONNY. You better believe it.

EDI. You're getting good use out of it, oh good. Isn't it gorgeous? It's the perfect size for a ladle, I thought.

LONNY. You don't even understand.

DANA. This one over here has been ladling like crazy.

LONNY. I can't put it down.

> *(***LONNY** *takes the ladle and starts scooping from one imaginary bowl into another. Then the doorbell rings.* **LONNY** *opens the door to reveal* **ALAN.***)*

ALAN. Holy shit, great wedding!

DANA. Right? I mean...

> *(***DANA** *hugs* **ALAN.** **ALAN** *notices* **EDI.***)*

ALAN. Look at you. You're enormous. Where's Paul?

EDI. Slammed with work.

ALAN. You guys get the blender?

DANA. Love the blender.

ALAN. It's the Margaritaville. Like the Buffet song. Maybe we crank that bad-boy up tonight.

LONNY. That was the plan.

DANA. Lonny, show Alan the ladle. *(To* **ALAN.***)* Edi got it for us.

ALAN. Oh yeah. You're gonna get some good use out of that.

EDI. You can use it for soups. Quinoa. Maybe a nice stew. If you ever make chili...

DANA. Do you guys want to sit down?

(They all head for the living room area.)

EDI. Mashed potatoes. Perfect for mashed potatoes. You know what you could use it for? Risotto! Anyway...

*(***EDI*** and ***ALAN*** take their seats on the couch. ***ALAN*** drops his keys on the coffee table. ***DANA*** and ***LONNY*** take notice and share a glance as they sit.)*

DANA. So... you had fun at the wedding...

EDI. Best wedding ever. It was perfect. And I'm not just saying that.

ALAN. Easily one of the best weekends of my adult life. I totally agree.

LONNY. Yeah, we're still coming off the high from it.

EDI. I mean, the food, the hotel, the Sunday morning fiesta...

ALAN. The burrito truck was out of control.

DANA. Yeah? You guys liked?

ALAN. A burrito that big, and that fresh? The ingredients were fresh. Only cost me like six bucks.

DANA. Well that's why we chose it. We wanted to have a Sunday event since everyone traveled so far to be there–

LONNY. But at the same time it had to be something everyone could afford.

EDI. The whole weekend was just so great. And so unconventional.

*(***DANA***'s hackles go up a little. She doesn't like criticism. And ***LONNY*** can't handle uncomfortable situations.)*

DANA. Unconventional? Like how so?

EDI. You guys did your own thing. You made it your own.

LONNY. But it was still conventional in the important ways.

EDI. It was a conventional wedding but you made it better. In a way, you fixed what's wrong with weddings. So thank you, guys.

(**DANA** *is now back on board.* **LONNY** *relaxes.*)

DANA. Well that's what we were going for. We wanted it to feel cool/cas, like not your typical wedding, but at the same time still have a hint of tradition.

LONNY. We wanted it to be about our friends and family.

DANA. Really a celebration of you guys.

EDI. That's what it felt like.

ALAN. It really did. Now whose idea was Sedona?

LONNY. I mean, those rocks.

EDI. So red.

DANA. And the best part, between us, is that it wasn't that expen–

LONNY. Let's just say, you can make your money go a long way in Sedona.

EDI. It was so lavish.

DANA. Are you kidding? We couldn't have done that wedding in LA.

LONNY. Dana was actually saying how the only downside of the wedding for her was that she couldn't also be a guest at it.

(**EDI** *and* **ALAN** *laugh a little too hard. Unable to resist any longer,* **DANA** *takes a coaster and carefully places it under Alan's keys.*)

ALAN. Oh. I'm sorry.

DANA. No, I'm sorry. It's new. We're crazy.

LONNY. It was expensive.

DANA. You'll never guess how much.

LONNY. No, it's okay. Go ahead. Guess.

EDI. I don't know. Four hundred?

*(**DANA** and **LONNY** start laughing.)*

LONNY. For that? We wish.   **DANA.** No, no... no, I don't
                                                      think so.

EDI. Four thousand?

DANA. Oh, come on, Edi. It's a coffee table.

LONNY. Thirteen hundred. It was thirteen hundred.

ALAN. Thirteen hundred. No shit.

DANA. Wasn't it just the wedding of a lifetime?

ALAN. That is a really nice table.

EDI. It's a nice table.

> *(A timer dings in the kitchen. **LONNY** hops up.)*

LONNY. The lasagna.

DANA. Back in a minute. Ooh, Alan – tell Edi your Costco story.

> *(**ALAN** laughs at the memory with **DANA** and **LONNY**, as they head into the kitchen.)*

EDI. What's your Costco story?

ALAN. We're not doing the Costco story.

> *(**ALAN** leisurely crosses to the kitchen doorway and listens for a beat. Then he returns to the couch and sits back down. He quietly turns to **EDI**.)*

So what'd you think of the wedding?

EDI. What'd *you* think of the wedding?

ALAN. Are they out of their minds?

EDI. Oh I am so happy to hear we're on the same page.

ALAN. Fucking Sedona. Are you fucking kidding me?

EDI. Well you can make your money go a long way in Sedona.

ALAN. First you have to get to Sedona. Pain in my ass.

EDI. Two planes plus a rental.

ALAN. I dropped five hundred on airfare so they could save on flowers. You realize we basically paid for their wedding.

EDI. Wedding of a lifetime? I'd love to know: Whose lifetime? Tell me whose lifetime.

ALAN. And can we talk about the chuppah?

On top of the mountain?

EDI. It was a thirty minute walk. I got shin splints.

ALAN. You can't make it black tie and ask me to hike it out. It's unacceptable.

>   (**EDI** *and* **ALAN** *abruptly look toward the kitchen, paranoid they've heard someone coming. Once* **EDI** *is completely sure they're in the clear, she turns back to* **ALAN.***)*

Did you get the welcome basket?

ALAN. I got a bag.

EDI. Yeah, the bag.

ALAN. A bag with a bottle of water, a chewy granola bar, and one Jolly Rancher.

EDI. You got a Jolly Rancher?

ALAN. How about those Friday night drinks?

EDI. Good thing I brought my wallet.

ALAN. I mean, are you shitting me?

EDI. The whole night would've cost them, what?

ALAN. Maybe seven hundred.

EDI. I thought they were doing well.

ALAN. *(Disappointed, shaking his head.)* I know.

>   (**LONNY** *pops in, drying his hands on a dish towel.* **ALAN** *and* **EDI** *immediately stop talking and shift their attitudes.)*

LONNY. You guys all good out here?

EDI. Excited for some 'sagna. Momma needs to eat.

>   (**LONNY** *leaves.* **ALAN** *turns to* **EDI**, *quietly.)*

ALAN. You still at the same number?

EDI. Call me tomorrow. We'll talk.

ALAN. Oh, you bet we will.

(**ALAN** *takes out his phone and starts texting.*
EDI *watches with slight disdain.*)

So what else? What... else...?

EDI. We found out it's a boy.

ALAN. *(Looking up, feigning enthusiasm.)* Oh my God...
(Back to phone.) That's, uh – you got a name yet?

EDI. Cary.

ALAN. *(Putting phone in pocket)* Gary. Nice. Classic.

EDI. Nope, nope. Cary.

ALAN. So it's like Gary but with a "C"?

EDI. It's literally the name Cary.

ALAN. We should say something.

EDI. Why would we do that?

ALAN. Because they're embarrassing themselves. Do you have any idea how many people hated that wedding?

EDI. Of course I do. I've been shit-talking this wedding all month.

ALAN. So what kind of friends are we, lying to their faces?

EDI. She'll start to cry.

ALAN. Yeah. She will. And that might be uncomfortable for *us*, but if we're actually the good friends we say we are, then we need to do what's best for them.

(**DANA** *comes in with a bottle of wine and sets it on the dining room table.*)

DANA. Oh my god, wait. Did you guys see Yosh at the wedding? When he got up on the table and started doing the running man...

EDI. Hilarious.

ALAN. Yosh!

DANA. I have a feeling that people are going to be talking about this wedding for a very, very long time.

(**DANA** *lets out a long sigh and then exits.*
EDI'*s smile drops as she looks back to* **ALAN**.)

ALAN. My sister and I are brutally honest with each other.

And sometimes it's tough to hear the truth. We yell and we scream, but we get through it, and we're the better for it. You see this head of hair? It's extremely thick. You know why? Because she sat my ass down and told me I was balding. It hurt at first. I was pissed. But then I took a good look in the mirror and I realized: she's right. So I took care of it.

EDI. Propecia?

ALAN. Steroid injections. Right in the scalp.

EDI. That's your family. Your family can't go anywhere. But if you talk to your friends like you do your family, I can promise you this... you won't have friends anymore.

> (**DANA** *and* **LONNY** *[holding a salad bowl] enter and cross to the dining table.* **ALAN** *and* **EDI** *move to join them.*)

DANA. What are you guys talking about in here?

ALAN. Babies! They picked out a name.

EDI. We're going with Cary.

ALAN. It's like Gary, but with a "C." It's genius.

> (*They all sit as* **LONNY** *starts serving salad, using Edi's ladle.*)

EDI. Oh! For salad. I didn't even think...

LONNY. So, really funny thing about the caterer–

DANA. We honestly didn't know the food was going to be as good as it was.

LONNY. But just like everything else–

DANA. It came together.

LONNY. We have been to so many bad weddings.

DANA. Who hasn't?

LONNY. Remember Steve and Michelle's wedding? Oh my god.

DANA. That wedding was the worst.

LONNY. So number one priority for us? Throw the best friggin' party anyone has ever been to.

DANA. Make it the wedding of a lifetime.

(*Everyone but* **ALAN** *takes a bite of salad. As they all chew and enjoy their food,* **ALAN** *puts down his fork and leans back in his chair, fighting the urge to say something. Just when it seems like he might speak, he stops himself. He struggles for a few long moments, until finally...*)

ALAN. And was it?

DANA. Was it what?

ALAN. The wedding of a lifetime.

DANA. Didn't you think so?

ALAN. I thought it was all right.

(**LONNY** *laughs.* **DANA**'s *blood pressure spikes a little.*)

DANA. What do you mean?

LONNY. He's joking, babe.

DANA. I don't get it. I don't get the joke.

EDI. (*Shoveling food into her mouth.*) Could someone please pass the salt? Not that it needs any.

ALAN. I'm just going to be honest with you because we've all been friends for so long and I know I'd want you to be honest with me. You won't be offended, right?

DANA. We can take it, Alan. We're adults.

ALAN. It was a selfish wedding.

DANA. That is so offensive.

ALAN. Here's the thing: in order for a wedding to be unselfish, more than just the bride and groom have to enjoy it.

DANA. You didn't enjoy our wedding?

ALAN. Not particularly. No.

DANA. Well luckily you were only one out of about two hundred extremely satisfied guests.

ALAN. Edi. Do you have something you'd like to say?

EDI. I thought it was a very strong wedding.

ALAN. She's a liar. (*To* **EDI**.) You're a liar.

EDI. Okay, fine... There might have been some issues.

DANA. Issues? *(Losing it.)* Get the fuck out of my house.

LONNY. *(Putting a hand on* **DANA.***)* No, babe. It's okay. Let's hear them out.

ALAN. *(To* **EDI.***)* Should we start with the Friday night drinks?

EDI. Maybe we start with Sedona.

ALAN. Really? I mean, I kind of feel like we cap it with Sedona.

LONNY. Hold up. You guys didn't like Sedona?

ALAN. It cost me five hundred dollars to get there.

EDI. We had to take off from work.

LONNY. But the rocks.

ALAN. Lonny. No one cares about the rocks.

> *(***LONNY*** stands up and starts to pace. This has really rattled him.)*

DANA. Sorry we're not millionaires. Sorry we're not fancy. Doing it out of town was the only way we could afford a wedding like that.

EDI. It was cheaper for you.

DANA. Yes.

ALAN. Wasn't cheaper for us.

LONNY. At least fifty people told me they thought Sedona was a great idea.

ALAN. They lied.

DANA. So you're mad because you had to spend a little more money than you would have liked. Well, you know what? Get over it. That's the deal, kemosabe. That's what happens when you go to a destination wedding.

LONNY. Yeah, guys. That's what happens when you...

> *(***LONNY*** abruptly turns upstage. There's a beat while they wait for him to finish his thought.)*

DANA. Oh, no.

ALAN. Lonny?

EDI. Is he crying?

DANA. Goddammit!

ALAN. *(Sotto, to* **EDI.***)* This is surprising. Because you thought that she would be the one...

LONNY. *(Fighting tears.)* I'm not crying. And I don't regret Sedona. Not for one minute.

>*(Still facing upstage,* **LONNY** *exits sideways into the kitchen trying to conceal his emotion.)*

ALAN. Should we continue?

EDI. We don't want to have to repeat ourselves.

ALAN. What else are we going to talk about?

>*(***EDI** *considers this and then turns to* **DANA.***)*

EDI. So the hotel situation.

DANA. Situation?

ALAN. There was only one place to stay.

EDI. It was like three hundred a night.

DANA. We gave you another option.

ALAN. The hostel? I'm a grown fucking man.

EDI. I'm pregnant. I'm gonna hop into a bunk bed?

DANA. Why is that our problem?

ALAN. And, by the way, what about the alcohol?

DANA. What about it?

ALAN. Where was it? Where was the liquor?

DANA. There was wine.

ALAN. One bottle per table.

DANA. We didn't think people needed to get wasted to have a good time.

EDI. At your wedding they did.

>*(***LONNY** *walks back in with conviction.)*

LONNY. The DJ was fantastic! Everybody loved the DJ!

ALAN. You mean the kid with the iPod? Yeah, I thought he put together a pretty good playlist.

> *(Defeated,* **LONNY** *goes right back into the kitchen.)*

EDI. We will admit the food was good.

ALAN. The food was good.

EDI. Obviously you saved money by doing it buffet style.

DANA. Okay.

> **(DANA** *gets up and starts dumping the salad from their plates back into the bowl.)*

ALAN. But it was good.

EDI. It was good.

LONNY. *(Off stage.)* People went crazy for that chicken!

ALAN. We liked the chicken, Lon. But you know where I've had better chicken? In Los Angeles. Where I live.

> **(LONNY** *comes back in.)*

LONNY. I don't understand why you're doing this to us. What did we ever do to you? Why are you being so mean?

> **(DANA** *takes their plates into the kitchen.)*

ALAN. We're trying to help you.

EDI. We just thought–

LONNY. Why are you bashing our wedding? Our wedding was amazing. It was a dream. Why are you saying it wasn't? I don't understand. I don't understand what's happening here, babe.

ALAN. Your wedding was terrible, Lon.

EDI. But to be fair, most weddings are terrible.

ALAN. No, that's true. But yours was the worst.

EDI. You think it was worse than Steve and Michelle's?

ALAN. I think it's close and I'll tell you why. I felt like at Steve and Michelle's, at least the vows were moving.

EDI. No, that's a good point.

LONNY. You weren't moved by our vows?

ALAN. Well you didn't really... I mean, you read a poem.

EDI. You didn't even memorize it, Lon.

ALAN. Was it a good poem? Maybe. But that's pretty subjective, I think.

(**DANA** *enters from the kitchen.*)

DANA. I thought you were our friends.

ALAN. That's exactly why we're telling you.

LONNY. To what end? For what purpose? What do you want from us?

ALAN. I mean...an apology would be nice.

DANA. Go fuck yourself, Alan.

LONNY. Oh, I'm really starting to get it now. Yeah, you bet I am. It all just snapped into focus, crystal clear. You're not doing this for us. You're doing this for you.

DANA. Because Alan just has to be right. Alan has to teach everyone a fucking lesson.

LONNY. Alan has to be big dog.

ALAN. Alan wants his money.

LONNY. What?

ALAN. You owe me a thousand dollars.

DANA. Oh, give me a break.

ALAN. You owe me a thousand dollars and a Margaritaville blender.

(**DANA** *and* **LONNY** *glance at each other. After a beat,* **ALAN** *puts it together.*)

Where's my blender?

LONNY. Just calm down.

ALAN. Where is my blender?

(**ALAN** *stands and heads for the kitchen.* **LONNY** *moves to stop him.*)

LONNY. Don't you go in there.

(**ALAN** *exits into the kitchen.*)

ALAN. Where is it, Lonny?!

LONNY. *(Calling after.)* It's in the shop!

> *(We hear cabinets opening and shutting in the kitchen.)*

It broke, okay? It broke because we were using it too much. We had to take it in to get it fixed. We didn't tell you because we didn't want you to be embarrassed.

DANA. We didn't want to hurt your feelings. Because we have manners.

EDI. You returned his blender.

ALAN. *(Storming in.)* You returned my blender!

LONNY. We don't drink margaritas.

DANA. It wasn't on the registry, Alan!

ALAN. That's another three hundred bucks.

DANA. Oh, shut the fuck up.

LONNY. It was a really nice wedding!

ALAN. I'm serious. I want my money. You owe me thirteen hundred dollars.

DANA. Well, good luck getting it.

> *(**DANA** and **LONNY** stand there defiantly, staring at **ALAN**. **ALAN** stares back. Finally, **ALAN** gives up. He heads for the front door, and opens it. Then he quickly turns back and makes a move for the coffee table. He swipes the coasters off of it and hoists it in the air. Struggling with the cumbersome table, he heads back to the door.)*

No! No! You put that down, Alan.

LONNY. Yeah, put it down, Alan.

> *(Once he gets to the door, he realizes that the table doesn't fit through the opening so easily.)*

ALAN. Edi! A hand!

> *(**EDI** gets up and heads over.)*

DANA. Do something, Lonny!

LONNY. What am I supposed to do?!

DANA. I don't know! Get the table!

> (**EDI** *squats and lifts the other end of the table. She and* **ALAN** *struggle to fit it through the door.*)

ALAN. *(To* **EDI***.)* Careful, careful... To the left. Edi, your left.

LONNY.	**ALAN.**
You better stop that, Alan. I'm serious.	Careful, Edi, you're gonna scratch it. No one wins if you scratch it.
DANA.	
He's serious, Alan!	Let's bring it back towards you...
LONNY.	
He's not stopping, babe. Why isn't he stopping?	Very good... and a little more to the left... Honey, it's always going to be *your* left.
DANA.	
Alan, you cut it out!	Around the corner. Easy, careful.
LONNY.	
Please don't do this to us. I'm begging you.	We're almost through aaaaaand... I got it from here.

ALAN. Really great seeing you.

EDI. You too!

ALAN. Love to Paul.

> (**ALAN** *exits with the table.* **EDI** *turns back to* **DANA** *and* **LONNY,** *who do not make eye contact with her. She's not quite sure what to do. Finally, she speaks.*)

EDI. Do you guys maybe just want to cut me a check or...

> (**DANA** *and* **LONNY** *are unresponsive.* **EDI** *tries*

to formulate what to say. Finally, she just gives up and exits, gently pulling the door shut behind her.)

*(**DANA** and **LONNY** stand there for a long beat, dumbstruck.)*

LONNY. You really think our wedding sucked?

DANA. They're both just very unhappy people. They'll figure it out.

*(**LONNY** and **DANA** sit down at the dining room table, trying their best to shake the whole thing off and forget everything that was just said. **DANA** serves them both salad from the salad bowl.)*

LONNY. Hey, babe. Who got us this salad bowl?

DANA. Steve and Michelle.

LONNY. That was nice.

DANA. That was nice. We should have them over next weekend.

LONNY. Yeah. They loved the wedding.

(A celebratory song kicks in, as Dana and Lonny chew their food, and the lights fade to black.)

End of Play